OLD STORMALONG
THE SEAFARING SAILOR

by
Carol Beach York

illustrated by
Paul Harvey

Folk Tales of America

Troll Associates

PROLOGUE

Nobody likes to tell a tall tale more than a sailing man.

A *tall tale* is a story stretched a little past the truth; stretched a little *too* far to be real.

But it's fun to listen to.

Sometimes these tall tales tell about folk heroes, people who do just a little more than anyone else and do it just a little bit better.

Of all the tall tales about the sea, none can beat the Old Stormalong stories.

It's true that they're stretched more than a little past the truth, a little bit *too* far to be real.

But they're fun to listen to. And fun to read about.

Copyright © 1980 by Troll Associates, Mahwah, N.J.

Library of Congress # 79-66322
ISBN 0-89375-314-9/0-89375-313-0 (pb)

Stormalong was born on a farm on the rocky coast of New England. The first sound he heard was the sound of ocean waves pounding on the shore.

The rugged New England coast was hard land to farm, and lots of folks took to the sea instead. But no one took to the sea like Alfred Bulltop Stormalong—"Stormy" for short.

5

He not only took to the sea, but he didn't waste any time about it. When he was only three years old, he lugged his mother's washtub down to the shore and set off into the ocean.

The washtub bounced over the waves, and who knows how far Stormy might have gone—if he hadn't stood up. Even at three years old, he was too big for the washtub. When he stood up, the tub turned over and dumped him out.

"I need a bigger ship," Stormalong told his mother.

"You don't need any ship at all," his mother scolded. Her washtub had floated out to sea, and she didn't feel very cheerful.

"That boy must have salt sea water in his veins instead of blood," his father said. Stormy's father was a true farmer—a true landlubber, and as firm as an oak tree. He didn't take to ships and sailing. Rough water made him seasick.

If Stormy did have salt water in his veins instead of blood, it didn't slow his growth any. You could see in half a glance that he was a strong, sturdy boy. And you might say Stormy "grew like a weed." Except no weed ever grew as fast as Stormy did.

He was too big for the school desks. On the very first day, he had to sit on the schoolroom floor to do his lessons.

He outgrew his clothes faster than his mother could sew new ones. Every time she finished a pair of britches for Stormy, she'd start right in making a larger pair.

"My needle and thread never get a rest," she said to Stormy's father.

But there wasn't anything Stormy's father could do about that. He couldn't stop Stormy from growing.

By the time Stormy was ten years old, he was a fathom tall and still rising. A fathom is how sailors measure the depth of the sea. One fathom is the same as six feet, or more than two and a half meters. So you can see that young Stormy was pretty big.

Because of his size, Stormy was a danger in the hen house, tramping about in his oversized boots. But he was strong enough to pull stumps when it came time to clear a field for plowing. And he could split logs twice as fast as anybody else, because he swung an ax in each hand.

"If you just stay away from the chickens, you'll make a good farmer," his father said.

Yet Stormalong never wanted anything but to go to sea. The high seas, the seven seas, the wide seas, the wild seas. Wind in the rigging and sea gulls circling overhead.

Stormy was one of America's BIG folk heroes. By the time he was ten and a half, he was bumping his head on the cabin ceiling. At bedtime he had to sleep with his feet sticking out the door—which wasn't much fun on cold winter nights.

When Stormy could sneak away from his farm chores, he liked to sit around the White Sail Inn, listening to the sailors swap sea stories. Mostly they were "tall" tales, stories that stretched the truth a mite, so to speak.

If you could believe the sailors at the White Sail Inn, they caught whales bigger than six ships tied in a row.

They got shoved all the way around Africa by high winds and had to fight off fierce wild animals.

They could all eat twenty steaks at one sitting.

Or so they said.

As you can see, the stories stretched the truth a bit. Sometimes they skipped over the truth entirely.

But Stormy loved all their yarns. He sat on the floor near the fireplace, toasting his toes. He smiled as he listened to the rough seamen

who had been to China and Russia and far-off places like that.

When Stormy got home, he liked to tell all he had heard at the White Sail Inn.

"You can't believe those tales," his mother scolded. She shook her head and pressed her lips together. "And don't be hanging around there with those sailors. Goodness knows what they'll be telling you next."

Mrs. Stormalong didn't hold with sailors. And she didn't think the White Sail Inn was the place for her little boy.

But Stormalong wasn't exactly what you'd call a "little" boy. He had never really been "little," even when he was a baby. But now he was twelve years old, and as tall as two grown men, so he decided to sign aboard ship as a cabin boy.

When he brought home the news, his mother threw up her hands!

"Can't you stop this foolishness?" she begged her husband.

But no one could stop Alfred Bulltop Stormalong. Not then or ever. His father was sorry to see his son leave, but it was plain to see that the boy was too big for the farm cabin. Too big for the school desk and the church pew. And too big for the hen house. Stormy needed room. He needed the wide sea and the high sky.

And he needed a bigger ship than a washtub.

Stormy's first real ship was called the *Sea Wing*. It was bound for China with a full cargo of furs and hides from the trappers of the new land of America.

It took a long time to get to China. During the voyage, Stormy grew another fathom. So he wasn't much good as a cabin boy. He kept bumping his head on the ship ceilings. The sailors call them "overheads."

"I was a dang fool to hire that young man," the captain muttered to himself as Stormy banged around. "That lad needs a bigger ship. And I'll tell him so when we get to China."

The captain rubbed his chin and thought some more.

"In fact, I'll dump him off there, before he capsizes my whole ship. Let China worry about him."

That was a pretty mean trick the captain had in mind. But while the *Sea Wing* was still off the coast of China, a heavy fog came down.

The captain was in his cabin, and he didn't like what he heard. Or to put it another way, he didn't like what he *didn't* hear.

He didn't hear the foghorn blowing.

He didn't hear anything but the slap of waves on the sides of the ship.

And he sure couldn't *see* anything with the thick fog all around.

"What's the matter with that foghorn?" he roared. "Give 'er a blast, mates, before we run into every other ship afloat!"

But it was so foggy that nobody aboard could see where the foghorn was.

It looked like a bad time ahead.

Until Alfred Bulltop Stormalong began to bellow. He bellowed like a foghorn, and he didn't let up all night long.

The next morning when the fog lifted, even the crusty old captain had to admit that Stormy had saved his ship. It gave him some second thoughts about dumping Stormy in China. But he still thought he might.

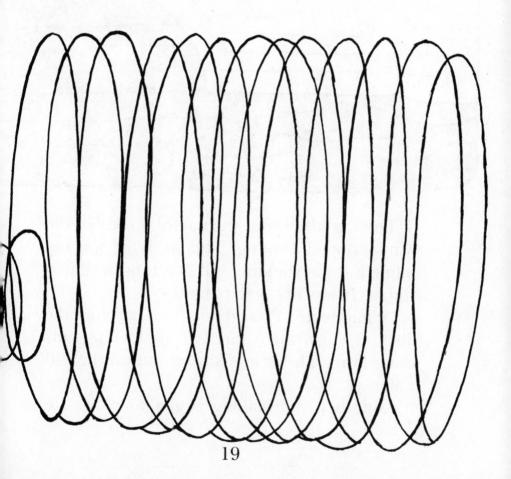

The fog lifted. But then all of a sudden the wind stopped blowing. The *Sea Wing* was becalmed. It was standing still. It was not going to China. It was not going anywhere.

"What next?" The captain paced around the deck. He growled and frowned. The sails hung limp. The sailors looked out on the still water.

And then Stormalong began to blow. He

20

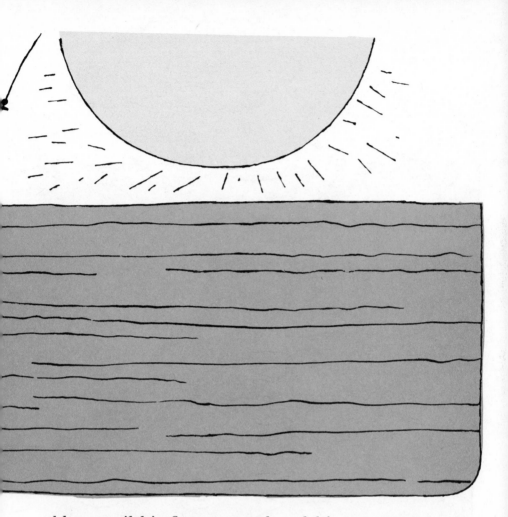

blew until his face was red and his eyes were popping. And he never let up all day long. The sails filled with air, and the *Sea Wing* sailed right into the China harbor, pretty as you please.

Well, that made up the captain's mind. Stormalong never knew what a narrow escape he had. He might have been left behind in China, and he couldn't even speak Chinese!

The captain let Stormy stay aboard for the voyage home. The ship was carrying silks and teas back to America. The people building log cabins in the wilderness were happy to get goods like these.

The crew had a grand celebration when they dropped anchor at home. They piled into the White Sail Inn, calling for hot drinks.

Even the captain joined the party. He told the innkeeper to give Stormy all the food he wanted.

"Captain," Stormy said, "this is a real treat."

"You saved the *Sea Wing*, lad. Twice. And I'm grateful to you."

The captain *was* grateful. But, even so, he had bad news to break. The bad news was that Stormy wouldn't be going on the next voyage of the *Sea Wing*.

"You need a bigger ship, lad," the captain said. "Bigger than mine."

You might think Stormy was upset, but he wasn't. He knew the captain was right. He did need a bigger ship. And that was the plain truth.

"To a bigger ship!" Stormy shouted. The rafters of the White Sail Inn rang. Sailors clanked their hot, steaming mugs.

"A bigger ship for the foghorn!"
"A bigger ship for Stormy!"

You could hear the commotion for a mile around.

The bigger ship that Stormalong found was the warship of Captain John Paul Jones himself. It was bigger than the schooner carrying furs and hides to China.

The American Revolution had begun. The colonies were fighting England, and John Paul Jones had brought together a fleet of ships. It was America's first navy. Captain Jones knew right away that Alfred Bulltop Stormalong was just the man he needed. He took Stormalong on board his own ship, the *Poor Richard*. It was the smartest thing that John Paul Jones ever did!

25

Stormalong helped Captain Jones to win the Revolution, in one victorious battle after another. And the greatest of them all was between the *Poor Richard* and the *Serapis*.

The *Serapis* was the headship of the English Navy. That meant it was the best—the biggest, the toughest, and the fastest. The most dangerous ship England had afloat. The *Serapis* had more deck guns and cannons than you could count, and when the *Serapis* met the *Poor Richard,* every gun began to blast.

The *Poor Richard* would have been done for on the spot. It was sinking fast. But Stormalong threw out a heavy rope and lashed it to the *Serapis*'s mainsail. That kept the *Poor Richard* afloat while Stormy fired his own cannon and forced the *Serapis* to surrender.

"I don't know what we would have done without you, Stormalong," Captain Jones said.

John Paul Jones usually liked to take credit for victories himself. For he was a very good sea captain, indeed. But this time there was no way around it. Stormy had beaten the *Serapis* and saved the *Poor Richard.* And Captain Jones had to admit it.

The Revolution didn't last forever. It only *seemed* as if it lasted forever. But finally the colonies were free. They became the United States of America.

The liberty bell rang.

It was a good sound to hear, but Stormalong wanted to hear ship bells and the creak of masts in a high wind. The trouble was, Captain Jones didn't need his warships anymore. So Stormalong was out of a job.

He thought about going back to his father's farm. He thought about pulling stumps and splitting logs and scaring chickens. But he just couldn't stay ashore.

Instead, Alfred Bulltop Stormalong hunted up the biggest whaling ship he could find, and he signed up to be a whaler. Now *that* was really something. With Stormy abroad on the seas, there wasn't a whale safe anywhere. He'd catch seven or eight little ones before breakfast, and then he was just getting started. Stormalong drank shark soup by the tubful, ate mackerel steaks and dried cod, and swallowed oysters, shell and all.

"A good breakfast puts life in a person," he would say. And then, as an afternoon pastime, he'd hunt out the biggest whale in all the ocean.

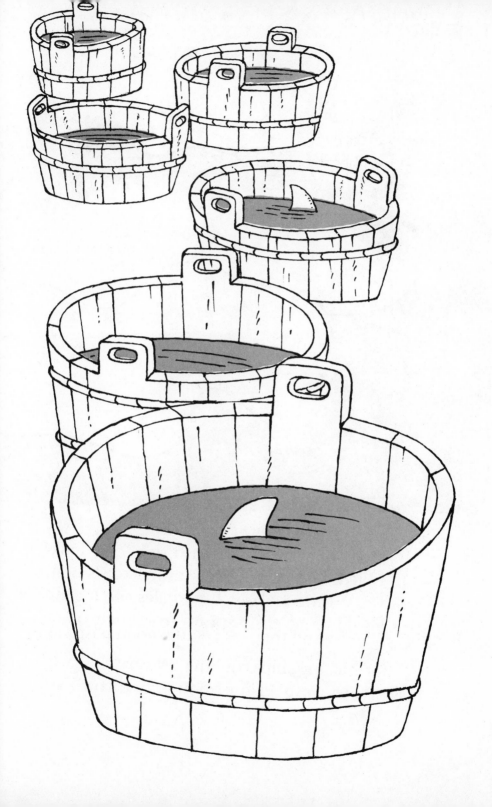

Only one whale ever got away.

"Thar she blows! Starboard side!" the lookout called, high above deck in the crow's nest. He was on the lookout for whales coming up for air, blowing misty sprays from their blowholes.

But whaling ships couldn't get very close to a big whale. To get close enough to throw har-

poons, the men had to set out in small boats.
So that's what Stormy did.

"Thar she blows! Starboard side!"

Stormy grabbed his harpoon, lowered a
boat, and rowed to meet the whale. With a full
red beard and a yellow tablecloth for a neck
scarf, he was a sight to see, slapping his oars
into the waves.

But the whale didn't hang around to take a second look. He swam for his life. And the faster the whale swam away, the faster Stormalong rowed after him.

Even when Stormy let loose with his harpoon, the whale kept going. Dragging the harpoon and the rowboat and Old Stormalong behind him at a furious pace.

Stormy hung on.

And hung on.

And hung on.

When the harpoon line broke at last, Stormy had a five-day swim back to his ship.

"Blast my sails and hatches," he cried. "I'm not going out to harpoon whales in those dinky boats again."

But nothing could keep Stormalong down. The next day, he went ashore and ate four shark steaks and a ten-gallon pail of clam chowder. He ordered six new shirts sewed up, and he waded back out to the whaling ship carrying his duffel bag over his head.

"I'm back, mates," he called as he climbed aboard. "And I'm not harpooning whales in those dinky boats again."

"You can't catch 'em any other way." The old-time whalers laughed at Stormy. "You can't get close enough."

"I'll just throw my harpoon farther," Stormy said.

"Nobody can throw a harpoon *that* far."

But Stormalong had made up his mind. He practiced and practiced, and pretty soon he could throw the harpoon and rope five times as far as anyone else. So he never had to leave

the big ship again. He'd just stand by the rail and let the harpoon rip.

"No whale is taking me for a sea ride again!"

And no whale ever did.

As the years went by, stories about Stormy and his sea adventures spread far and wide:

"Old Stormalong finally found a ship so big the first mate rides a horse around the deck to give out orders!"

"Stormy found a ship so big he's the only one who can turn the wheel. If he's not there, it takes ten sailors!"

"Stormy found a ship so big he can't get into port. He has to drop anchor in mid-ocean!"

At every sailors' inn, the tales were told.

And no one liked to tell them better than Stormalong himself. He had listened to sailors' stories when he was a boy. Now when the seamen gathered beside the fireplace at the White Sail Inn, Alfred Bulltop Stormalong had his own share of tales to tell.

His red beard had turned to white now. His skin was burned dark from the sun and the sea wind. But his blue eyes were as sharp as ever. And nobody could tell a story the way he could.

He liked to tell about the English Channel and the cliffs of Dover!

"*Mateys, my ship was so big, there was only one way to get through that skinny channel. 'All hands look alive,' I shouted. 'Overboard with you! Soap up the sides, and we'll slip through like a greased eel on a tin plate!'*"

As many times as they heard the story, the sailors always laughed.

Stormalong's ship slipped through the English Channel all right. But all that soap rubbed off onto the cliffs, and it dried there. And that's why the cliffs of Dover came to be called the White Cliffs of Dover after that.

And Stormy liked to tell about the Panama Canal.

Of course, there wasn't any Panama Canal until the night Old Stormalong's ship got swept off course by a storm.

"We sailed right through on dry land," Stormy said. "Digging up that canal as we went. All sails full."

Stormy slapped his knee and chuckled as he remembered that historic night.

And he told about his first voyage. It was one of his own favorite stories.

"I had my first ship when I was only a boy of three."

"Three years old!" The sailors were surprised. Some of them even said, "Ho, ho! That can't be."

"It can be and it was," Stormalong declared.

"And what kind of ship was it?"

Stormalong paused a moment. He didn't exactly want to mention that it was his mother's washtub.

"It was a fine, sturdy craft," he finally said. "But it wasn't big enough for me. Even though I was only three years old, I needed a bigger ship. I've always needed a bigger ship."

"A bigger ship for Old Stormalong!" the sailors yelled. The hot, steaming mugs clattered. The fire leaped high. "A bigger ship for Old Stormalong!"

"Aye, mates," Stormalong said with a laugh, "a bigger ship for me!"